The Adventures of Goliath

Goliath on Vacation

The Adventures of Goliath
Goliath on Vacation

Terrance Dicks
Illustrated by
Valerie Littlewood

BARRON'S
New York

First edition for the United States and
the Philippines published 1987 by Barron's
Educational Series, Inc.

First published 1985 by Piccadilly Press Ltd.,
London, England

All inquiries should be addressed to:
Barron's Educational Series, Inc.
250 Wireless Boulevard
Hauppauge, New York 11788

Library of Congress Catalog Card No. 86-28895

International Standard Book No. 8120-3821-5 (pbk.)

International Standard Book No. 8120-5824-0 (hardcover)

Library of Congress Cataloging-in-Publication Data

Dicks, Terrance.
Goliath on vacation.

(The Adventures of Goliath)
Summary: Lovable Goliath disrupts hotel life when
David and his parents go on vacation, but the big dog
redeems himself by helping solve a mystery of disappearing ponies.
[1. Dogs—Fiction.   2. Mystery and detective stories]
I. Littlewood, Valerie, ill.   II. Title.   III. Series:
Dicks, Terrance. Adventures of Goliath.
PZ7.D5627Gu 1987   [E]   86-28895
ISBN 0-8120-3821-5 (pbk.)
ISBN 0-8120-5824-0 (hc.)

PRINTED IN THE UNITED STATES OF AMERICA

789   977   987654321

CONTENTS

Chapter One

Vacation Hotel

"WOOF! WOOF! WOOF!"
Goliath's crashing barks seemed
to shake the hotel dining room.

Plates jumped. Glasses rattled.
Even the windows seemed to shake.

All the people eating breakfast
turned and stared.

"WOOF!" Goliath barked again,
louder than ever.

The waiter jumped about a foot
in the air and dropped the tray.

1

Bacon, sausages, toast, and
fried eggs shot everywhere.

Goliath was overjoyed.

He'd only been hoping for a
sausage or two. It was very kind of
the nice man to give him the whole
tray.

But if Goliath was happy, a lot of other people were not.

Unhappiest of all were the three people sitting at the table in the corner, wishing they were invisible.

David, Goliath's owner, and his mother and father. The most embarrassed of the three was David himself.

He was the one who'd persuaded his parents Goliath could be trusted in a hotel.

A vacation in a hotel was a new experience for David and his family. Usually they went on some kind of do-it-yourself holiday, renting a seaside cottage or a camper.

*   *   *

This year David's mother had rebelled.

3

"It's all right for you two!" she said. "But what about me? All it means is I get a chance to do cooking and housework in a different kitchen!"

David and his dad looked uneasily at each other.

They did help with the jobs, both at home and on vacation. But they knew it was David's mom who ended up doing most of the work.

"Can't we go camping again?" asked David hopefully.

"What? After last time?"

"Just because Goliath got frightened by those cows in the night and ran away . . ."

"It's not his running away I minded," said David's mother. "It's the fact that he took most of the tent with him! No, this year I want

4

a real bed and a roof over my head and someone else to cook the meals and do the dish washing. I want to stay in a *hotel*."

"What about Goliath?" demanded David.

"He'll have to go to a boarding kennel," said David's father. "Your mom's quite right, she deserves a real vacation. And you can't expect a hotel to put up with Goliath!"

"It's not fair," grumbled David. "Goliath deserves a holiday, too!" He just knew Goliath would hate being put in a kennel.

Next evening after supper David produced a book and handed it to his father. "Here you are, Dad."

His father looked at it. " 'Family Hotel Guide.' What's all this?"

"I got it out of the school library," explained David.

"Thanks a lot, son, that'll be really helpful." His father flicked through the book. "There seem to be quite a few nice places here."

"That's right, there are," said David. And he added casually, "Quite a lot of them say, 'Dogs Welcome.'"

That wasn't the end of it, of course. It took quite a lot of argument and persuasion after that.

Finally, David got his parents to agree that Goliath could come with them.

After all, he pointed out, it was actually cheaper to take him, since the extra you had to pay for bringing a dog was much less than the cost of putting him in a kennel.

It only remained to decide where they should all go.

After a lot of discussion, they finally decided on the New Forest.

It was easy to get to, it was close to the sea, and there were lots of things to see and do.

Above all, there were the famous New Forest ponies.

*   *   *

So now here they all were—and already David was beginning to suspect that his parents had been right.

Goliath just wasn't made for hotel life.

He was too big, too clumsy, and too scatterbrained.

They'd run into trouble on the very first night.

It had turned out that you weren't actually supposed to have your dog in your room with you. There were special kennels at the back of the hotel.

The trouble started when the hotel people discovered they didn't have a kennel big enough for Goliath. So they dug out an old mattress and said Goliath could sleep on that.

Unfortunately, Goliath, for all his size, was rather timid. He didn't care for being left on his own with a lot of strange dogs.

When Goliath was unhappy, he howled. Great, wailing, "Hound-of-the-Baskervilles" howls that echoed through the entire hotel.

Naturally, all the other dogs howled in sympathy, and soon

agitated dogowners were getting up
in their bathrobes and hurrying
down to the kennels, to see what
was wrong with their beloved pets.

Goliath stopped howling as soon
as David appeared. But as soon as
David started to leave, he started
again.

David turned to the manager,
"It's no good, I'm afraid. Goliath has

always slept in my room, ever since he was a puppy. Either I sleep here, or Goliath sleeps with me."

The thought of one of his guests sleeping in the kennels hurt the manager's professional pride. He said Goliath could sleep in David's room.

David had a tiny, single-bedded room on the same floor as his parents. They lugged Goliath's mattress up there and put it on the floor beside David's bed.

Next morning they all got up and went down to breakfast in the big dining room, leaving Goliath shut in David's bedroom.

Unfortunately, the chambermaid had opened the door to tidy the room. Goliath promptly shot past her and went looking for David.

Attracted as always by the smell of food, Goliath made his way to the dining room—where he had the unfortunate encounter with the waiter . . .

To David's relief, everyone was amazingly nice about it. Waiters and waitresses came running to clear up the mess, and the manager, a tall handsome man who looked like a movie star, patted Goliath on the head and told David and his parents not to worry.

The only one who wasn't nice was the man in dark glasses at the table by the window—the one whose bacon, eggs, and sausages Goliath was happily eating.

He made the most *enormous* fuss. "It is disgraceful!" he shouted. "An animal that size should not be allowed in the hotel. First it keeps everyone awake, and then it causes chaos in the dining room. I insist that the animal and its owners be asked to leave the hotel at once."

David looked at his parents in horror.

It looked as if their vacation was going to be over before it was really started.

Chapter Two

The Sinister Millionaire

To David's delight, the manager stuck up for them—and for Goliath.

He looked down at the angry customer. "I am very sorry that your breakfast was delayed, Sir. But this is a family hotel, a place for parents, children—and dogs. From time to time these little incidents will occur."

The man began spluttering.

Smoothly the manager went on, "There are several hotels in the neighborhood where neither dogs nor children are allowed. If you wish to transfer we should quite understand."

The man in dark glasses calmed down with amazing speed. "Oh, never mind," he grumbled. "Where's my breakfast?"

Another waiter appeared with a tray. "Right here, Sir."

He began serving a fresh helping of bacon, eggs, and sausages, and the manager moved to David's table.

"I'm very sorry about all this," said David's father. "Perhaps we ought to leave. We seem to have offended one of your best customers."

"Not one of our best— one of our worst," said the manager, lowering his voice. "Mr. Nexos comes here every year about this time. And every year he complains about the noise and the children—and the dogs."

"Who is he?" asked David. "Why does he come here if he doesn't like it?"

"I believe he is very, *very* rich," said the manager disdainfully. "As to why he comes here, I have no idea. He is rude to the staff, uncivil to the guests, and sometimes he has friends to visit him, flashy, unpleasant people like himself."

As soon as breakfast was over, they collected Goliath and set off to see the New Forest.

David and Goliath sat in the back
of the car. David was reading the
guide book, and Goliath, as usual,
insisted on sticking his head out of
the window.

David and his parents were
delighted with the New
Forest— even though, as the guide
book said, it wasn't really new, and
it wasn't a forest either.

In fact it was a mixture of forest
and a sort of open heathland.

The real attraction of the New

Forest was the ponies. They were everywhere, in scattered little groups, standing in the shade of the trees at the forest edge, and wandering along the sides of the narrow roads.

The ponies seemed to come in all shapes and sizes, from the quite large to the very small. Quite a lot of the ponies had foals, delightful creatures with big eyes and long, spindly legs.

But it wasn't only in the country that the ponies took over. As David discovered when they came back to the hotel and parked the car to do some shopping, the ponies were just as much at home in the local village as well.

As they walked along the busy little main street, David was

astonished to see a pony and foal standing right in the middle of the sidewalk with the shoppers edging their way round them.

The mother was a beautiful chestnut color, but the foal was pure white.

David stared at it in astonishment and delight, and Goliath on his leash beside him was even more surprised.

He peered at the foal in amazement, wondering if it was some new kind of dog. He gave it a friendly sniff, wagging his tail, and the mother whickered in alarm.

"I'd keep the dog well away, son, if I were you," said a voice beside him. "The mares can be a bit touchy when they've got foals with them."

David turned and saw a nice looking old man in a corduroy suit. He was sitting on a bench on the village green. He had a brown wrinkled face like a country apple, and a soft country burr in his voice.

David pulled Goliath away. "He wouldn't hurt the foal, he's only curious. I think he thinks it's a new kind of dog."

The old man chuckled. "Well, that dog's big enough to be mistaken for a new kind of horse!"

"How come the donkeys and ponies are just wandering about loose?" asked David. "Are they strays? Don't they belong to anyone?"

"Why, of course they do. Local farmers like me, mostly. Every one of those ponies is marked and registered and every so often they're rounded up for the sales." The old man pointed. "That white foal there now, he's mine. He's called Snowy. Fetch a good price when he's a bit older he will, those pure white ones are very rare."

David's parents came out of the shop and stood chatting. The old man's name was Dan Bowyer.

As David and his parents said

good-bye and moved away, a red convertible sports car came down the street. It was honking impatiently and driving much too fast, and several shoppers had to jump out of the way.

David looked up as the car went past.

Behind the wheel was the unpleasant Mr. Nexos from the hotel, with an even more unpleasant-looking man beside him, scruffy and red-faced with a bushy mustache.

Mr. Nexos had been staring very hard in their direction.

For a moment David thought he'd recognized him and was still angry about his breakfast.

Then he realized that Mr. Nexos had been staring at the white foal.

The car disappeared down the street.

David watched it go. "That's funny," he thought. "He didn't seem like the sort of man to be fond of animals."

But Mr. Nexos *had* been interested, thought David. And he had been particularly interested in the little white foal called Snowy.

After finishing their shopping, David and his parents went on with their tour, driving slowly around the forest and over the patches of open heathland, getting out to walk around, and looking for riding stables for David.

This took longer than they expected, and they were just about to turn back when David spotted a weathered sign at the bottom of an even narrower lane leading off the one they were in: *Riding Stables* "There's one," he called.

David's father looked down the tiny rutted patch. "I can't get the car down there. I'll park here, David, you go and ask."

David got out of the car, Goliath leaped out of the car after him, and they set off down the path.

David opened the gate, and they went inside. The whole place looked shabby and run down, and it seemed to be deserted.

David looked inside one of the stables. Inside were a couple of shaggy brown New Forest ponies, stretched out on some straw. They seemed to be asleep.

Behind him a gruff voice shouted, "Hey, you!"

David turned and saw a burly,
unshaven man come out of the
house and come pounding across
the cobbles toward him. He wore
dirty jeans and a grimy blue shirt
with no collar, and he was
clutching a half-eaten pork chop in
one hand.

The man advanced menacingly
toward David. "What do you think
you're doing?"

"Just looking around," said David

calmly. "I wanted to ask if there was any chance of a ride."

"Ride?" said the man as if he'd never heard of such a thing.

"That's right. This is a riding stable, isn't it?"

"Closed," muttered the man. "Out-of-season."

David shrugged. "All right. What's the matter with those ponies in there? Are they ill?"

The man grabbed David's arm in a painful grip. "Spying, are you?"

Suddenly, Goliath streaked across the yard and jumped up at the man with a tremendous "Woof!"

The man let go of David's arm and sprawled over backwards.

Goliath stood over him and barked again, while David looked at him in astonishment.

What had got into Goliath? he thought.

Then he noticed the direction of Goliath's eyes. They were fixed on the pork chop in the man's hand.

Goliath hadn't been rushing to the rescue after all. He'd just been thinking about food as usual.

Luckily, the man on the ground didn't know that. "All right, all right," he yelled. "Call him off."

Grabbing Goliath's collar, David dragged him out of the yard.

He went back to the car and said briefly, "No good, the place is closed down."

"What was all that barking and yelling?" asked his mother.

"Oh, just Goliath being silly," said David. "Let's look for somewhere else."

As they drove away, David heard another car coming along the lane behind them.

He looked out of the back window and was just in time to see a red sports car turning into the lane. "Look, it's that Mr. Nexos again. He keeps popping up everywhere."

Chapter Three

Goliath Disappears

Next day David and Goliath were up and about bright and early.

After all the rushing around yesterday, David's parents had decided to spend a quiet day in and around the hotel.

After breakfast David's parents sat out at a table on the hotel terrace, drinking coffee and reading the morning papers.

David took Goliath off to explore, promising faithfully to be back in time for lunch.

He decided to start with the hotel grounds, which were so large as to be almost a park in themselves.

David and Goliath had a fine time, stalking each other around the winding paths, hiding and jumping out on each other from behind bushes.

Hide-and-seek was one of Goliath's favorite games. Not that he was very good at it. He got too excited to stay still when he was supposed to be hiding, and always gave himself away by barking loudly. David was teaching him to "play dead," to give him a better chance.

They had been playing for some time, and it was David's turn to hide. Telling Goliath to "Stay! Play dead!" David ran off, turned a corner, and hid himself inside a particularly thick and prickly holly bush. You had to be careful, but there was a space at the very center you could wriggle into.

David crouched down in hiding. "Ready!" he shouted. He grinned to himself as he heard Goliath jump up, bark, and go crashing off in exactly the wrong direction.

David decided to wait a bit longer before putting Goliath out of his misery. Just as he was about to come out, he heard footsteps and voices coming toward him.

One voice was flat and cold, with a hint of a foreign accent.

The other was hoarse and thick, with a country twang.

David peeped through the leaves—it was Mr. Nexos, and with him was the red-faced man who'd been in the car.

"Remember," Mr. Nexos was saying, "twenty animals, no more."

"I could just as well make it fifty," growled the countryman.

"More than twenty would be dangerous. It is not worth the risk. But those twenty must be the best, mind you. Every one perfect. And I must have the white one . . . Leave it till last, it will be missed."

David must have shifted position without realizing it, because the red-faced man suddenly cocked his head. "There's someone in that bush!"

He sprang forward, crashing through the leaves, and grabbed David by the shirt collar, and dragged him out.

"You!" snapped Mr. Nexos. "Why were you spying on us? What did you hear?"

"I wasn't spying and I didn't hear anything," said David, telling at least half the truth. "I was playing hide-and-seek with my dog, and you just happened to come by . . ." He tried to wriggle free, but the man tightened his grip, looking at Mr. Nexos. "What do you think?"

"It is possible, I suppose. The boy is staying at the hotel . . ." Mr. Nexos reached out and took David's shoulder in a painful grip. "You were listening to a confidential business conversation. If you know what's good for you, you will keep your mouth shut, and you will keep well away from me. Do you understand?" And he shook David hard.

Once again it was Goliath who saved the day, and once again it was for all the wrong reasons.

Goliath hurtled through the air above him, slammed into Mr. Nexos, and sent him crashing into the center of the bush.

The other man gave a yell of alarm and set off at a run.

David and Goliath ran, too—in the other direction.

They sprinted back to the hotel terrace and sat down beside David's parents, who seemed to be on their third or fourth cup of coffee.

"My, you're out of breath," said David's mother. "Have you had a nice game?"

David nodded, too out of breath to speak, and Goliath threw himself down, panting and lolling out his long pink tongue.

They had lunch in the hotel and then, feeling as David's dad said a bit too stuffed, they decided to walk it off.

David put Goliath on his leash, and they all strolled down to the village, stopping on the way to admire the little groups of ponies.

David was keeping an eye out for the white foal that they'd seen the day before, but there was no sign of it.

They did see Dan Bowyer again, though, and stopped for a chat.

"We were hoping to see Snowy again," said David. "I suppose he's off in the forest somewhere?"

The old man looked grave. "I dunno where he is," he said. "That's a mystery that is. Look!"

He pointed to the other side of the road. The chestnut mare, Snowy's mother, was trotting along the side of the road, her head turning from side to side.

"She's been up and down this

main street a hundred times," said
Dan Bowyer. "I reckon Snowy's
lost, and she's a-looking for him,
see?"

Suddenly, David knew exactly
what Mr. Nexos's mysterious
business was.

*   *   *

David was silent and preoccupied over dinner. Who could he tell of his suspicions?

Suddenly, he realized his mother was speaking to him. "So, will you be all right, David, if we go?"

He stared at her. "Go where?"

His father sighed. "The boy's in a dream. Your mother's just finished explaining that there's a dinner dance at the hotel tonight, and she and I have decided to get ourselves all dressed up and go."

"We haven't been to a dance for years," said his mother happily. Then she looked anxious. "But will you be able to look after yourself for the evening?"

"Oh, yes, you go. I'll be fine. I'll take Goliath for a nice long walk and tire him out. Then maybe I'll be able to get some sleep tonight."

David said good-night to his parents and left them happily getting ready for the dance.

Then he went along the hall to his own room to pick up Goliath.

But Goliath was gone.

Instead, there was Mr. Nexos, sitting on David's bed.

As David stood staring in astonishment, Mr. Nexos leaped up and pulled him into the room and slammed the door, standing with his back to it. "Now listen to me, little boy," he began.

David interrupted him. "Where's Goliath? What have you done with him?"

"Listen!" said Mr. Nexos again. "I am not sure how much you

overheard, or how much you have guessed about my affairs. But remember this. Your dog is—missing. Tomorrow, provided I have concluded my business without interruptions, your dog will reappear. He will just turn up, early tomorrow morning, in the hotel again. But if you breathe one word to anyone, if you cause me any trouble—then I promise you, you will never see your dog again."

Chapter Four

David to the Rescue

Mr. Nexos opened the door and slipped out, closing it quietly behind him.

David sat down on his bed. For a moment he was stunned. What should he do? Obey Mr. Nexos, keep quiet, and hope Goliath would be returned?

It didn't take David long to decide against this. He didn't trust Mr. Nexos one little bit. Once his mysterious business was over, why should he even bother to keep his promise? Much simpler to . . .

David shuddered and got to his feet. No, he couldn't take that risk. He had to get Goliath back himself —tonight. Luckily, David had one big advantage—something Mr. Nexos didn't suspect.

Grabbing his jacket, David left the room and hurried along the hall and down the stairs.

David ran out of the hotel and down the road that led to the village.

David was very relieved to find old Dan Bowyer sitting on his usual bench on the village green.

He ran up to him, panting. "Mr. Bowyer, you've got to help me. Someone's been stealing ponies.

They've stolen your white foal, and
my dog as well. And I know where
they are!"

*   *   *

David crept silently up to the gate
of the abandoned riding stables.
Dusk was beginning to fall, and
the trees rustled eerily in the
evening breeze.

Holding his breath, David crept into the cobbled yard. He stopped in amazement.

Standing in the center of the yard was an enormous semitrailer. It was a wonder how they'd managed to get it in there at all.

David crept around the edge of the truck and began looking over the half-doors into the stables.

They were all empty.

The drugged ponies had disappeared—and David had a pretty good idea where they were.

They were in that semitrailer, with lots of others, ready to be shipped overseas.

David looked into the last stable and found that this one wasn't empty.

A white shape was lying on the

straw in a shadowy corner.

For a moment David thought he'd found Goliath.

Then he realized.

It wasn't Goliath at all.

It was Snowy. For some reason, the thieves hadn't loaded the little white foal onto the van.

David thought fast.

He went into the stable and lifted up the foal.

It was surprisingly heavy, but he just managed to carry it in his arms.

He staggered across the yard with it and laid it gently on the grass under the wall just to one side of the gate.

Then he went back into the yard. Snowy was rescued, but he still had to find Goliath.

As he went back into the yard he
heard a low, rumbling, snorting
sound, a sound David knew well.
It was Goliath snoring.

The sound came from a sort of

office at the far end of the row of stables.

Goliath was curled up on the floor of the office, sound asleep. Or perhaps he was drugged, thought David with sudden alarm. Then he saw the almost untouched bowl of dog food beside Goliath.

No doubt they'd put the drug in that. But Goliath hadn't eaten more than a mouthful—just enough to make him a bit dozy.

Goliath was very fussy about his food. The only brand he would touch was "Wuffo, Builder of Champions."

David whispered, "Hey you! Psst! Wake up, you great lump."

Goliath opened his eyes, stared blearily at David, then opened his mouth to bark a welcome.

"Sssh!" hissed David.

Goliath gave him a hurt and puzzled look, but he didn't bark.

David heaved him out of the office and into the end stable.

Suddenly, the front door of the house on the other side of the yard swung open.

Light streamed out, and the red-faced, bushy-mustached man appeared. He paused and spoke to someone still inside. "Hadn't we better load that foal with the others?"

A voice said, "No, leave him where he is. I'll put him in the Land Rover and drive him to the airport. He's being flown out for a very special customer."

It was the voice of Mr. Nexos.

The first man said, "I'll just

check he's okay, then."

To his horror David heard footsteps approaching the stable. If they found out Snowy was gone . . .

Ducking behind a bale of hay in the corner, David whispered, "Quick, Goliath, dead dog!"

Obediently, Goliath flopped down and lay still.

A shadowy figure appeared in the gap at the top of the half-door. It peered at the white shape on the straw and called, "Looks okay to me!"

Good old Goliath, thought David. Just keep still a minute.

Then to his horror he heard Mr. Nexos call, "Wait! You might as well put him in the Land Rover now. I'll be leaving soon."

The stable door opened, and the man came in and picked Goliath up.

It took him a minute to realize he wasn't carrying a very small pony, but a very big dog.

He dropped Goliath with a yell of alarm. "The foal's gone—and that big dog's loose!" He ran toward the house.

Goliath followed him, barking furiously, anxious to join in the new game.

David ran after him—and saw Mr. Nexos and the man who owned the stables running toward him.

"I'll deal with these two," shouted Mr. Nexos. "You two get the truck away!"

The two men leaped into the truck, and one of them started it up. But before it could get going, a white police car with a flashing light on top roared up the lane and swung across the gates, blocking the entrance.

Lots of reassuringly large men in blue jumped out, followed by old Dan Bowyer.

Help had arrived at last.

*   *   *

It was all mopping up and explanations after that.

Mr. Nexos and his gang had been visiting the New Forest for several years now, stealing the best of the ponies and smuggling them abroad to wealthy and unscrupulous buyers, using the half-abandoned riding stables as their headquarters, and its owner as their accomplice.

But they wouldn't be doing it anymore.

David and Goliath were interviewed by a local journalist, and Goliath got his picture in the papers again.

The headlines over the picture

read, *Dog Detective Saves Pony Pals.*

David grinned when he saw it. They were on the hotel terrace, drinking coffee—soda for David.

Once again, Goliath was getting all the credit, thought David. But David didn't mind. He was just happy he'd got Goliath back. He hugged Goliath till he grunted.

David's dad said, "Now perhaps we can get on with our vacation!"

And so they did.

Other *Adventures of Goliath* that you will enjoy reading:

Goliath and The Burglar
Goliath and The Buried Treasure
Goliath at The Dog Show

About the author

After studying at Cambridge, Terrance Dicks became
an advertising copy-writer, then a radio and television
scriptwriter and script editor. His career as a
children's author began with the *Dr Who* series and he
has now written a variety of other books on subjects
ranging from horror to detection.

More Fun, Mystery, And Adventure With Goliath –

Goliath And The Burglar
The first Goliath story tells how David persuades his parents to buy him a puppy. When Goliath grows very big it appears that he might have to leave the household. David is worried—until a burglar enters the house, and Goliath becomes a hero! (Paperback, ISBN 3820-7—Hardcover, ISBN 5823-2)

Goliath And The Buried Treasure
When Goliath discovers how much fun it is to dig holes, both he and David get into trouble with the neighbors. Meanwhile, building developers have plans that will destroy the city park—until Goliath's skill at digging transforms him into the most unlikely hero in town! (Paperback, ISBN 3819-3—Hardcover, ISBN 5822-4)

Goliath On Vacation
David persuades his parents to bring Goliath with them on vacation—but the big hound quickly disrupts life at the hotel. Goliath is in trouble with David's parents, but he soon redeems himself when he helps David solve the mystery of the disappearing ponies. (Paperback, ISBN 3821-5—Hardcover, ISBN 5824-0)

Goliath At The Dog Show
What chance would a mongrel like Goliath have at winning a ribbon at the dog show? On show day, Goliath's canine friend Nipper disappears. Then Goliath mysteriously misbehaves and adds to the show's confusion. But David's huge dog helps solve these mysteries—then wins a prize! (Paperback, ISBN 3818-5—Hardcover, ISBN 5821-6)

Goliath's Christmas
Snow before Christmas means fun for David and Goliath, but the cold means trouble for Miss Gorringer, David's elderly neighbor. David sends Goliath looking for her—and together they rescue her, in time to enjoy the best Christmas party ever! (Paperback, ISBN 3878-9—Hardcover, ISBN 5843-7)

Written by Terrance Dicks and illustrated by Valerie Littlewood, all of the Goliath adventures are at your bookstore or available directly from Barron's for just $2.95 each in paperback, $4.95 each in hardcover. When ordering direct from Barron's, please indicate ISBN number and add 10% postage and handling (minimum $1.50). N.Y. residents add sales tax.

250 Wireless Boulevard, Hauppauge, N.Y. 11788
Call toll-free: 1-800-645-3476, in NY 1-800-257-5729